Emoji Adventures #1

The Horse Party

BONUS!

We have a FREE Book waiting for you...
www.montagepublishing.com/free-book-club

ISBN 978-0692651025

#ALittleAboutMe

I've lived in Emojiville my whole life. I'm pretty good at playing the piano, but I should be since Mom's the only piano teacher in town.

I also love horses. My bedroom and locker are covered in horse posters - one poster spells out ANNIE in tiny horseshoes which my Mom picked up at a yard sale.

You can probably tell by my smiling face that I'm pretty optimistic and happy most of the time. I'm not saying I'm ALWAYS happy but when billions of people around the world use your image to convey how happy they are, I spend a lot of time PRETENDING to be. My parents, my teachers, my friends - everyone expects good old Annie to look on the bright side.

I try my best.

I wonder if it's something other kids struggle with too: how to be yourself while being what other people expect you to be.

#MyFriends

My best friend Dorothy, aka Dot, lives down the street. Maybe it's because she's an only child, but she and I are like sisters. Dot is the smartest person I know - always beating me in board games and tests at school. She plays forward on the soccer team and is one of the best players in the league.

One of the bad things about Dot is that she gets ten crushes a day.

When we have a new substitute teacher, she's unbearable. I've seen her go gaga over a glitter pencil. (I ought to know, it was my glitter pencil she was obsessed with until I finally gave it to her to shut up.) Unfortunately, the person she goes kookiest over is my twin brother, Kevin. If I could've given her Kevin along with the glitter pencil, believe me, I would have.

My other best friend is Billy. He moved in across the street when I was in preschool and we've been friends ever since. His two older brothers boss him around all the time, so he always ropes us into pranking them as revenge. Billy loves animals and wants to be a veterinarian. His dog, Taylor, just had puppies so Dot and I have been spending a lot of time at Billy's house.

The three of us do everything together - soccer, art, movies. Next weekend the fair is in town and we'll be going to that as well.

I guess you could say Dot, Billy, and I are MILDLY popular. Not loners like Craig or Lynda, but not as popular as Tiffany and her crew who are at the top of the Emojiville social food chain.

 Everything about Tiffany is perfect: her great clothes, her schoolwork, her life. I do, however, think the tiara's a bit much. No matter what Tiffany says, a tiara is not appropriate for P.E.

Tiffany is never without her loyal subjects, Austin and Zoe. Because Austin always charms the teachers, he gets away with wearing sunglasses in class. He swears they're prescription, but everyone knows they're not.

Zoe is a good artist and the goalie on our soccer team. But I think the real reason Tiffany hangs out with her 24/7 is that she laughs at pretty much everything Tiffany says. No- she laughs at pretty much everything ANYONE says. I think it's kind of annoying but we've won a lot of tournaments with her as goalie so I don't complain.

I don't mean to be negative - as I said, being positive and upbeat is kind of my thing. But sometimes it's hard to stay happy all the time, isn't it?

#MyFamily

My brother Kevin and I are twins. People usually don't believe we are, because we look and act NOTHING alike. Lots of kids say their brother is the devil, but mine IS one. Literally.

He is also pretty remarkable with robotics. No other kid in town can program and build robots like Kevin. Unfortunately for me, what he usually programs his robot, SAM, to do is hide my phone. It wasn't funny the first time he did it, never mind the hundredth time. He even named his robot SAM, short for Sister Annoying Machine.

Even though Kevin looks like a devil, he can be kind and giving when he wants to be. But when someone choses to say something mischievous in a text, it's the image of my brother's face they use.

If you're wondering how everyone in Emojiville got into your phones, it's the work of one person - my Dad.

Dad's had a million money-making schemes, most of which totally bombed. (You still can't bring up the baby cage without Mom dying of embarrassment.) But his idea to license the images of our city's residents is by far his biggest success. Who knew billions of people on the planet would rather talk in pictures than words? My dad, that's who.

It's just a coincidence that Kevin and I are often at the top of the lists of Dad's emoji tracker. I wish my popularity here in Emojiville was reflected by how often I'm used on strangers' phones, but unfortunately that's not the case.

Everyone in Emojiville is grateful for Dad's idea since the licensing money paid for upgrading all the parks, schools, and roads in our town. Dad still has lots of ideas, but now they're pretty much all about emojis.

Mom used to teach music at Emoji High, but now she gives private piano lessons. Kids from my school are constantly coming in and out of my house. If you think that Mom knowing every kid in town and Dad making all of us rich would make me the most popular kid at school, you'd be wrong. Apparently neither of those things are as important as a tiara.

We adopted our cat, Freckles, when he was just a kitten. He used to be wild, but got used to the indoor life pretty fast. Now he sleeps with me every night and only goes outside when he's with me.

Tonight Mom made a casserole, but looking at the chunks of eggplant and mystery meat has me second guessing how hungry I am. Kevin insists on eating leftover pizza, and of course, Whatever Kevin wants, Kevin gets. He pulls the pepperoni and cheese off with his fingers and swallows it without chewing.

"Kevin, use your silverware." Mom goes into her speech on the value of table manners.

As I push the chunks of food around my plate, I use my famous optimism to make a wish. Tiffany's been talking about her party all week and I hope, hope, HOPE I'll be invited. I love my friends; I love my family. But it would be GREAT to be invited to the giant blow out party held by the most popular girl at school. Tiffany said she was handing invitations out tomorrow. (I wasn't eavesdropping, just listening as she spoke to Austin and Zoe in the hall.) I reach into my pocket to check the date and realize my phone is gone.

"Mom, Kevin took my phone again!"

Mom shakes her head. "This is between the two of you - it has nothing to do with me."

Kevin scarfs down another gob of cheese.

"Tell me where it is!"

Kevin ignores me and keeps eating.

It takes several minutes for me to find it - hidden in the slot of the toaster.

"Someone could've made toast!" I yell. "My phone would've melted!"

"No one makes toast at night," Kevin says. "It was totally safe."

Why did I get stuck with a devil twin?

#TheInvitation

Dot, Billy, and I take our seats in the back of math class and pull out our homework. A minute later Tiffany walks in, entourage in tow. Time slows down as if the entire class is now in slow motion. Tiffany's tiara sparkles like there's a Hollywood spotlight following her every move. Her professionally styled hair shines against her silver crown.

"Another perfect day for the perfect girl," I whisper to Dot. But she's too busy reviewing her homework to answer.

I turn to Billy and tell him the same.

"I heard you the first time," Billy says. "And yet I still don't care."

Tiffany stands in front of the class and pulls a stack of envelopes from her sparkling messenger bag. Straightening her tiara, she walks down the far row handing out invitations to her upcoming birthday party. My heart pounds with anticipation.

She smiles and jokes with our classmates as she passes them out.

When she finally arrives at my row, my palms sweat and I hope the invitation doesn't drop out of my slippery hands. She stops at the desk in front of me and hands Lars - the transfer student from The Netherlands - an invitation.

"A horse party," he says. "Sounds fun."

TIFFANY'S PARTY HAS A HORSE THEME? Now I HAVE to get invited. I play it cool and skim through my math book, pretending not to care. I can see Dot out of the corner of my eye, still reviewing her homework - oblivious to the social importance of this critical moment.

My heart sinks as Tiffany turns and walks back to her seat.

I turn to Billy but he puts his finger over his mouth before I can say a word.

The class chats about the upcoming party; not only will they be riding horses, it'll be held in a private section of the town fair! Tiffany beams with pride as Mr. Whittaker walks into the room.

I keep smiling even though I don't feel happy. Why wasn't I invited? I love horses! I know about every breed! It's hard to stay positive but I try my best.

"Settle down, class," our teacher says, "You can discuss the party later."

Even our teacher knows about the party! This isn't fair!

"Everyone pass forward your homework and pull out a pencil for a pop quiz."

I moan along with the rest of the class then stare at the first question:

$x = y - z$

If $2x = 4y$ what does z equal?

All I can think is that if

x = Party and y = Classmates

and z = Me

Party = Classmates - Me

"What did you get for question six?" Dot asks on our way to lunch.

"I didn't get that far."

"Are you serious?! It was a twenty question quiz."

"I couldn't concentrate," I respond. "All I could think about was that stupid party we didn't get invited to."

"What party?" Dot asks.

OMG!!

Both of my friends are completely unaware of the importance of this moment. When we get to my brother's locker, he's leaning against it with an armload of books.

Peeking out of his English textbook is an invitation.

"Hi, Kevin," Dot says. "You're doing a great job holding up that wall."

I roll my eyes at my lovestruck best friend and grab the invitation from Kevin's book. The envelope is covered in beautiful hand-drawn horses. "How did YOU get invited to Tiffany's party and not me?" I ask.

Kevin shoots me a mischievous smile. "Like I'm even going," he says. "Who cares?"

"I CARE!"

He grabs the envelope back. "This is how much I DON'T care." He puts down his books and holds out the invitation.

"NO!"

Kevin slowly rips the invitation in half and shoves it into the bottom of his locker on top of a pile of sweaty, stinky socks.

This means war.

#ALookInTheMirror

Popularity doesn't matter to Dot. She's in her own lovestruck world, happy to be playing soccer and hanging out with me. And don't get me started on Billy. It's incredible how he just laughs whenever someone makes a poop joke at his expense. I'd give anything to be as carefree as either of them.

I lay on my bed that evening with Freckles and stare at my favorite horse poster until Mom tells me to get ready for bed. I ask her for five more minutes.

She says okay and sits beside me. "I know Kevin can be a pain but you can't let it bother you. There's a lot to be said for having a positive attitude - you'll find that out as you get older."

She kisses my forehead, then gives me another five-minute warning before closing my door.

I hide my phone in my dirty clothes hamper where I know Kevin won't dare look then head to the bathroom.

You know that expression 'Nice guys finish last?' If that's true, why am I being so NICE all the time? So happy, so content? I'm tired of finishing last. My brother is an actual DEVIL and he gets invited to the party of the year and I don't? I'm definitely doing something wrong.

I stare at my reflection in the mirror. No more Miss Nice girl. No more Miss Happy All The Time. I'm going to get myself invited to Tiffany's party if it's the last thing I do.

Kevin pounds on the door. "Let me in before I pee in the hallway!"

I shut off the light and shove my way past my brother.

"What's YOUR problem?" he asks.

I ignore him and start putting together my Master Plan.

#LotsofIdeas

♫ Dot and Billy show up at my house after school, both eager to hear my plan. I'm just as eager to improve my pathetic social status.

"What if I have a theme song that plays wherever I go? It'll be stuck in everyone's head and Tiffany will *have* to invite me to the party."

"That idea stinks as bad as Billy," Dot says.

Billy starts to object, then shrugs.

"We need an idea that will get kids excited, not annoy them." Dot pulls out her tablet and syncs it with the TV. She opens a blank document and writes *Operation Party* across the top. She asks for suggestions just as SAM walks into the room.

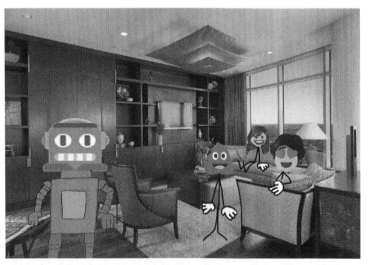

"What did the pen say to the pencil?" SAM pauses, then answers. "What's your point!"

I look at Dot and Billy and roll my eyes.

"Tough crowd," Kevin says from the other room. "Guess I should program better jokes."

"That's hilarious, Kevin!" Dot says. "You're really funny- I mean SO funny. You should have your own comedy show. I'd watch you all the time."

"I hate it when she gets like this," I whisper to Billy.

"Which is pretty much all the time."
He points to Dot who leans against the doorframe staring at Kevin.

 Dad pops into the room holding his laptop. "You kids like the idea of emoji pillows?"

"I don't want someone sleeping on my face!" Billy says.

"I don't think anyone wants to sleep on poop," Dot says.

I tell Dad I like the idea.

"Two out of three say no," Dad says into his laptop. When he turns, I notice a conference room full of business executives on the video conference call.

SAM grabs a banana from the fruit bowl and heads to the kitchen to give it to Kevin.

Seeing the fruit gives Billy an idea. "All kids love food - we could hire a food truck to come to school and make everyone hamburgers."

"The vegetarians will hate that." Dot returns to the couch. "How about an ice cream truck?"

Billy shakes his head. "People will end up thinking I'm chocolate soft-serve again."

Dad pops his head in one more time. "Emoji toilet paper?" he asks.

"No!" Dot says.

"Ewww!" Billy says.

"Gross!" I say.

"Three yeses over here!" Dad says enthusiastically into his laptop. "That's a surefire winner!"

I try to get us back on track. "I could make my grandmother's famous cookies."

Both Dot and Billy like the idea. Billy also suggests we bring his puppies to school to get the 'cute' vote.

In the next hour, we come up with lots of ideas - texting the class, magic tricks, a horse piñata, even skywriting.

We finally settle on our top three:

Plan A- Baking Cookies

Plan B- Puppy Party

Plan C- Ice Cream Truck

"One of these should get me invited to the party." I smile.

Dot and Billy look confused.

"Don't you mean get *US* invited to the party?" Dot asks.

That's what I meant, isn't it?

#FreeCookies

It takes almost the entire weekend to make enough cookies for every kid in my grade. (Several batches may have been burned - or spilled on the floor and eaten by Freckles.) Fortunately, Dot, Billy, Dad, and Mom step in to help. Even Kevin jumps in for a while to knead the dough.

"Your friends will love these."
Kevin controls SAM with his remote
to help us put the cookies in bags.

I guess being direct with Kevin
worked. No fake smile on my face, just a
simple question to see if he'd help. Chalk
up a victory to the new Annie. Maybe it's
possible for him *not* to be a devil if he
tries.

At school, Dot and I hand out the
cookies during lunch. I pass them out
with a real smile, saving Tiffany and her
friends for last.

My classmates are grateful for free
cookies and soon Dot and I are
surrounded by kids. Mason and Clark

fight over who gets Craig's cookie since he's not here today. Tiffany, Zoe, and Austin huddle at their table in the center of the cafeteria, occasionally glancing my way.

Kevin gives me a thumbs up from his table across the room.

Next stop - Popularity Central.

I walk towards Tiffany's table, almost bumping into Mason spitting his cookie into the trash. (My mother was right about manners. If you prefer another flavor, Mason, use a napkin next time.)

I approach Tiffany and the other popular kids.

"I was baking cookies for my Mom and thought I'd also bake some for the class." I hold out the tray of cookies. "It's my grandmother's famous recipe."

Austin purposely drops his cookie on the floor "Oops, mine broke. I'm sure it was great, though."

"Too bad I don't like peanut butter," Zoe says.

"They're chocolate chip."

"Did I say peanut butter? I meant chocolate chip." Zoe leans back and tosses hers in a nearby trash can.

With her friends looking on, Tiffany takes a bite of the cookie.

"It tastes...crunchy." Tiffany spits the cookie into her napkin. "Now I see why this recipe is famous - that's the worst cookie I've ever had."

Zoe laughs at the not-even-a-joke and hands Tiffany a water bottle.

I feel a tap on my shoulder and turn to see Dot and Billy.

"Your gorgeous brother must have sabotaged these," Dot whispers in my ear. "They're full of kitty litter instead of sugar!"

"I could tell the moment I took a bite," Billy says. "Acme Super Litter to be exact."

I watch my classmates all throw their cookies into the trash. I catch a glimpse of Elizabeth who quickly looks away, Mason and Clark push the extra cookie toward each other, as if they're playing air hockey.

WHERE IS MY BROTHER?!

When I finally find him, he's at a table laughing with his friends.

OF COURSE he had no intention of helping me! Why did I think he was on my side? Shouldn't I know better by now?

I put my head down and hurry toward the door. My face gets hot as the laughter in the cafeteria grows louder.

I hurry into the girls' room and hide in one of the stalls. I wanted to get invited to the popular kid's party, is that so bad? I wanted to ride a horse, okay? I spent all weekend making cookies - why am I the laughing stock of the whole school?

I spend the rest of lunch hiding where my popularity is - in the toilet.

#MyEvilTwin

 I race home after school to get to Mom before Kevin does. Good old happy Annie would've taken today's disaster lying down, but not new Annie. Now that I'm trying to express ALL my emotions, I'm ready to let anger take center stage.

Mom makes me wait until Mrs. Lee is finished practicing her scales before letting me launch into what I now refer to as the Kitty Litter Cookie Fiasco. I describe the incident in painstaking detail while Mom takes food out of the fridge to start making dinner.

When I finally finish, she just shrugs. "Are you sure it was kitty litter? Did Kevin say how it happened?"

"I know it was kitty litter because Billy said it was. And Billy is an expert."

"I'm sure there's a reasonable explanation," Mom says. "Maybe Kevin got the bags of sugar and kitty litter confused. He IS dyslexic."

I stare at her in disbelief. "NO ONE CONFUSES SUGAR WITH KITTY LITTER! Suppose he put some in the sugar bowl?

I bet you and Dad wouldn't think kitty litter in your coffee was so funny, would you?"

It feels like steam is coming out of my ears. When you're happy 99% of the time, anger certainly feels strange.

Kevin strolls into the kitchen carrying his skateboard and grabs an apple from the bowl.

"Well?" I ask. "Would you like to apologize for ruining my life?"

"Remember, I sent you a video last time I apologized - that way you can replay it whenever you need to hear one."

"Kevin, I don't know how you keep up with all this technology," Mom says. "Maybe you can look at my laptop - the screen keeps flickering."

"Sure, Mom. No problem."

"That's it?" I ask her. "No punishment for trying to poison my classmates, not to mention my reputation?" I feel like I might cry but I'd never in a million years let Kevin see a single tear.

"Oh, Annie." She tousles my hair as she heads to the stove. "You're going to the fair with Dot and Billy this weekend, right? There's so much to be happy about - why focus on a slight mishap?"

"A SLIGHT MISHAP?!"

"Where's that nice smile?" Mom continues. "Come on, let's see it!"

I storm out of the kitchen and sit behind the piano. I bang out *Beethoven's Fifth* as loud and obnoxiously as I can until my hands hurt.

It takes me awhile to find my phone. (Kevin hid it inside Dad's toolbox.) I've received a dozen texts from Billy and Dot asking about Plan B.

Even a brother with evil super powers can't keep me from Tiffany's horse party.

#PuppiesOnParade

Billy tries to talk us into doing our Ice Cream Truck plan next, but I think it's only so he can convince our classmates that he really looks more like chocolate ice cream than poop. But Dot and I beg him to let us launch Operation Puptacular instead. He finally relents and we spend the rest of the afternoon getting the puppies ready.

"How are the puppies going to get to school?" Billy asks. "We can't take them on the bus."

"SAM should walk them over during recess!" Dot says. "A robot AND puppies will be doubly successful."

I tell her the only reason she wants to involve a robot is so she can see Kevin. And after the cookie disaster, that's not going to happen.

"A robot walking puppies to school would be amazing," Billy agrees.

After much debate, we decide that Billy will ask Kevin to borrow SAM for a school project, mentioning nothing about our puppy plan. Dot and I hide behind the garage as Kevin gives Billy the remote and shows him how to program SAM. It gives me a special pleasure knowing that my brother is clueless and that he'll be the reason I get invited to the best party on the planet.

"Rumor has it that Mr. Whittaker's out sick because of your cookies," Dot says.

"He didn't even have any!"

Billy sits down next to me and pulls out his smartphone. "The good news is - SAM's on the way. The remote Kevin gave me has a link to the GPS on my phone."

He holds it up and points out a red

dot on a map which is moving toward

the school.

"Your brother's a genius!" Dot says. "It's so sweet of him to show us how to program SAM."

I remind her that he has a lot of making up to do after a lifetime of torture.

The bell rings and Tiffany walks in with Austin and Zoe. I try to make eye contact as to say, *Sorry about those terrible cookies,* but none of them seem to notice I'm here.

The substitute math teacher walks in and informs us that Mr. Whittaker is on Jury Duty. Not killing a teacher is the only good thing that's happened so far today.

The sub asks where we left off and Dot answers immediately without raising her hand.

He thanks her and she nearly faints.

"No problem," Dot says, "Just let me know if you have any more questions."

I look at Billy who pretends to throw up.

Dot, Billy, and I race out the door when the bell rings. It's puppy time!

I ignore Kevin when I see him in the hall. (He's pretending to choke on a cookie while his friends laugh.)

We're the first to arrive in the cafeteria and grab a table on the patio.

Billy sets out a water dish for our canine guests.

"Look, a robot!" someone shouts.

"And puppies!"

"The robot is *walking* the puppies!"

Tiffany is the first to arrive at the gate.

"My plan is working!" I say.

"Your plan?*"* Dot and Billy say in unison.

"You know what I mean." I shrug and turn back to SAM.

"Must walk puppies," SAM says, repeating the phrase over and over.

Within minutes, the entire class surrounds the puppies, taking in their non-stop energy. Loving the attention, the puppies run from student to student. The crowd laughs, which gets the puppies even more excited. So excited that one of the puppies starts walking around in circles.

"Uh, oh," Billy says. "You know what that means."

After the dog poops, half the class laughs while the other half groans in disgust.

"Don't look at me." Billy points to his head.

Tiffany walks up to the table to get a better look at the puppies. Austin and Zoe follow close behind.

"I hope somebody's going to pick up that poop," Mrs. Zimmerman says.

I rummage through my lunch to find a bag as SAM whizzes by.

"Must remove poop." The robot turns from me, to Dot, to Billy.

"I don't know what he's doing." Billy frantically works the remote. "I can't control him anymore."

SAM stumbles from us to Mrs. Zimmerman to Zoe to Tiffany. His metal arm grabs the satin lunch tote from Tiffany's hand.

"My basil and portobello panini!" Tiffany cries.

The robot bends down and scoops up the dog's mess with Tiffany's lunch.

Not her designer lunch tote! It matches her tiara!

Everyone is silent as Tiffany stares at the robot holding her silver bag. Her gourmet panini and organic chips bounce around the bag alongside the poop.

OMG, not again!

"I don't know what happened!" Billy says. "It's as if...."

"Someone over-rode your remote?" I point to Kevin at the picnic table manipulating the robot with a second controller. He shoots me his most devilish smile.

I thrust my half-eaten lunch at Tiffany. "I'm so sorry! Please take mine!"

"No thanks." She turns to leave. "I lost my appetite."

"I hope you feel better for your horse party this weekend." As soon as the words come out of my mouth, I want to take them back.

"Way to go, loser!" Austin says.

Zoe chuckles as they follow Tiffany back inside.

I look around again for Kevin who just laughs.

Billy holds me back before I can pounce on my brother. "Can't blame me for the poop this time," he says.

"But you were laughing!"

"It was funny!" he responds, "P.S.-everyone else was too."

"Kevin would make a great bad guy on a tv show," Dot says dreamily. "He's a criminal mastermind!"

The bell rings and Principal Lopez breaks up the crowd, sending everyone to class. He hands me a rag and a bucket to clean up the mess. Dot and I leash up the puppies for their return trip home. Billy tries his remote which suddenly works again.

I can't wait to get home and rat on my brother so my parents can do nothing YET AGAIN.

#ABigSurprise

On the way to our soccer game after school, Dot and Billy do their best to cheer me up.

"Tiffany's stupid horse party is at the fair," Billy says. "The three of us are going anyway - you won't miss a thing!"

"We're not even friends with Tiffany," Dot adds. "I don't know why you want to go so bad."

Because it would be nice to be invited. Because I've never hung out with the popular kids. Because I love horses! But I don't say any of these, just stare out the window of Dad's van.

Today's game is against Emojiville Academy; last time we played them, we got killed. I'm surprised to see Kevin, SAM, and a few of his friends in the parking lot. Kevin just figured out how to program SAM to skateboard and is showing off to his friends. I'm SO glad Kevin quit soccer - at least now I can enjoy the games without worrying about someone on my own team tripping me.

Zoe stretches on the sidelines, hysterically laughing at Austin trying to juggle three cones. The weirdest thing about Tiffany ISN'T her tiara or the rhinestone-encrusted number on her uniform, it's the fact that she's walking towards me.

With an invitation.

I immediately begin my own stretching routine and tell myself to calm down.

"Annie," Tiffany says. "This is for you."

I ignore Coach's whistle and open the horse-themed envelope.

"My parents told me I could invite twenty kids max," Tiffany explains. "Someone didn't RSVP so I can invite one more."

My eternal smile gets a little wider. Of course the person who didn't RSVP was my lame brother who ripped the invitation in half. After all his efforts to foil my plans, I end up getting invited because of him!

I tell Tiffany I'll definitely be there; she says she'll pick me up Saturday at ten.

I'm going to hang with the popular kids! I'm going to ride horses! I tuck the invitation into my bag and sprint onto the field.

"Looks like our plans worked after all." Billy gestures to where Tiffany and I just stood. "Either that or the princess just took pity on us."

"What did she say when you told her you were already going to the fair with your friends?" Dot says. "Is she mad you're not going to her party?"

I run over to join Mason in warm up drills as I find the right words to answer Dot. "I thought I WOULD go," I finally say. "You guys don't care, right?"

Even though we're in the middle of warming up, Billy and Dot both stop running.

"All those ideas Billy and I had were for ALL of us to get invited - not just you. All for one, right?"

Billy agrees. "We didn't put in all that time so you'd bag us."

The coach yells from the sidelines for the three of us to get moving.

"We gave you those ideas because we're your friends, but all you care about are kids who AREN'T." Dot picks up the pace and sprints toward the ball.

"We're outta here!" Billy follows.

The game starts and Dot steals the ball shortly after kickoff and drives down the field past multiple defenders before expertly kicking the ball into the goal.

Several of our teammates high five her as she jogs back toward me.

The other team immediately calls a timeout.

"Have fun at the party with your new friends." Dot and Billy head to the sidelines, leaving me standing in the middle of the field alone.

#RadioSilence

I text Billy and Dot every hour until bed. Neither respond, but I can see they've both looked at my texts. I wake up late this morning to no messages.

Okay, I realize I MIGHT have given them the impression that I wanted all three of us to get invited to Tiffany's party. But if I'm honest, if I'd gotten an invitation on that first day in math class I would've gone to the party with or without Dot and Billy. Yes, they're my best friends, but is there anything wrong with exploring other groups of kids too? Dot and Billy just assumed these plans were for ALL of us to get invited. Does it make me a bad person if I only cared about me?

Brushing my teeth, I see Billy and Dot out my window leaving early for school. They've never been this mad. Not having Dot and Billy around gives me the same feeling I get when Kevin steals my phone- it's like my whole body knows something's missing. Even gloating to Kevin about me going to Tiffany's party instead of him gives me no satisfaction whatsoever. (Probably because Kevin still doesn't care one bit about the party.)

The school day goes by like time has slowed down. Every time I try to make eye contact with Billy or Dot, they turn away.

Tiffany passes out a handwritten note on beautiful Palomino paper with all the party details; I'm thrilled to be one of the kids getting one, of course, but the excitement is dampened by Dot and Billy's attitude. Why can't they just be happy for me?

At least I know I'll get to see them at lunch; Billy, Dot, and I have been sitting at the same table for years. But as I take out my lunch, I can't see them anywhere.

And then the unthinkable. I gaze out the cafeteria to see my two best friends playing tetherball in the schoolyard. The truth hurts - Dot and Billy would rather not eat at all than eat with me. I think about moving over to join Tiffany, Austin, and Zoe at their table but deep down I know I don't belong there.

I finish my lunch and hope that after tomorrow's party I will.

#HorseParty

I try on three different outfits but still can't decide which one's best. What if it's not elegant enough for Tiffany's taste? What if my outfit clashes with my horse?

I snap a selfie in my white blouse, brown vest, and pink cowboy hat and prepare to text it to Dot for her approval.

Except that Dot's not talking to me and I'm on my own.

"Are you sure you want to wear that?" Kevin asks. "You look like a rodeo clown."

I grab my balled up socks and throw them at him. All I succeed in doing is scaring Freckles.

"Don't forget your bedazzled spurs," he calls from the other room. SAM follows him down the hall looking like a bandit in black cowboy hat and bandana.

"Your ride's here!" Mom says. "And what a ride it is!"

I take one last look in the mirror and change into my patterned top before heading outside. Tiffany and Zoe pop their heads out the sunroof of the limo and wave.

My first limo ride!

"Howdy partner." Austin tips his hat and opens the limo door.

Zoe looks adorable in her fringed vest and skirt; Tiffany's cowboy hat is topped with a detachable tiara. (A bit much, even for Tiffany.)

Inside are more than a dozen kids excitedly talking over one another. I introduce myself to Tiffany's parents and take a seat between Fern and Fran, the

other twins in my grade.
People usually can't tell them
apart but if you look closely,
Fern always wears something pink while
Fran prefers purple.

"Ever been to a horse themed party
before?" I ask them.

"Yeah, when I was four." Fran rolls
her eyes.

I can't imagine NOT being excited
about horses.

The group conversation turns to
school gossip. It's fun talking about the
new volleyball coach and Violet's fight
with Nancy over which one will make the
cheerleading squad, but after awhile I

realize I don't care about most of what passes for news. I do laugh harder than anyone else at Austin's spot-on impersonation of my devilish brother.

After taking the back roads through Emojiville, the limo drops us off at the entrance to the fair. Tiffany leads us to the front of the line, passing everyone else in town on our way to the VIP entrance.

"No waiting in line for us!" Tiffany says.

Zoe laughs as if that's just hilarious and I'm embarrassed when I spot Dot and Billy in line. They don't smirk, they don't frown, just look at us blankly. I've spent the past few weeks trying to be part of this new group and now that I'm here, I almost want to be somewhere else.

Thankfully, we get to ride HORSES! The stable is decked out with balloons, streamers, and colorful birthday signs. I place my present - my favorite horse book series - on a table alongside a giant pile of other gifts. I hope Tiffany likes the books - and the glittery, fancy wrapping paper - considering I spent days agonizing over what to get her.

The nearby table contains trays of gourmet food from Emojiville's most upscale restaurant. Decorative labels lie in front of each with names like Goat Cheese Bruschetta, Pan Seared Tilapia, and Grilled Tofu. Where are the burgers and pizza?

"Everyone ready to ride?" A gruff cowboy with a thick brown moustache introduces himself as Buffalo Bill Cody. His partner wears a wide brimmed hat and tells us to call her Annie Oakley. I pull out my phone and snap a picture only to realize I have no one to text it to besides my parents.

Buffalo Bill and Annie Oakley walk us through the basics of horse riding safety, which I already know from watching hours of videos online.

I cut in front of the twins trying to get a better look at the horse before we head to the stable. *I'm about to ride my first horse!*

We each get to pick our own horses and I go back and forth before deciding on Jelly Bean, a beautiful five-year-old black mare who whinnies when I approach.

As I stroke her mane, I breathe in the smells of the barn and stare into her dark eyes. Is Annie Oakley going to teach us how to braid ribbons into their manes and tails? This is going to be the best party ever!

From the open window, I spot Dot and Billy playing carnival games on the midway. Billy is throwing darts, trying to upgrade his prize. Dot cheers him on, but pays closer attention to the teenage boy behind the counter than to Billy.

Looks like fun.

"Okay, kids, let's ride!" Buffalo Bill leads us out of the stable. The horses know the drill by heart, following each other one by one down the dusty trail.

Austin starts a chorus of 'Happy Birthday' to Tiffany and we all join in.

"Okay, kids, get ready to turn back!" Buffalo Bill says.

"Wait? What?!"

Surely this can't be it.

The horses obediently turn and head back to the stable.

"Alright, cowpokes," Buffalo Bill says, "Time to dismount and mosey over to the tent for tiara and belt buckle making."

Tiaras? Belt Buckles? I thought we were braiding tails and manes! I thought we could be cowgirls!

Inside the tent, Fran and Fern rave about the boring food they pretend to eat but stash under their seats.

Did I ditch my best friends for this?

A scream rings through the tent. Dot, Billy, Kevin, and SAM are jumping up and down, screaming at the prize Billy just won at the nearby dart game.

A life-size stuffed animal pony.

Even though I haven't talked to my BFFs in days, I know who Billy just tried so hard to win that prize for.

Me.

"Thanks so much for the great books," Tiffany says. "I can't wait to read them."

I tell Tiffany I'm glad she likes my present and I hope she has a very happy birthday.

Without me.

I say goodbye to Jelly Bean and race over to find my friends.

#LetsHaveSomeFun

 As I look for Dot and Billy on the midway, I hear a loud ding followed by cheers.

"I am a winner!" SAM's robotic voice says as the attendant hands Kevin yet another stuffed animal.

Just past him, I see Dot and Billy buying cotton candy. Billy holds the large pony he won at the dart game.

"Stop gloating," I say to Kevin as I pass, his arms full of prizes. "It's not like YOU won them."

I slow down as I approach Dot and Billy, unsure of what to say.

"Your awesome, amazing party done already?" Dot asks.

"Were the horses wearing tiaras too?" Billy adds.

"They only let us ride for ten minutes." I say.

Dot hits me with her stuffed animal and laughs. "You ditched us for a ten-minute pony ride?"

"We knew you wouldn't have that much fun," Billy says. "You should've seen

Kevin freak out when SAM stepped in a cow patty."

They laugh when I tell them about Austin's hilarious impersonation of Kevin.

"Being at the fair isn't as much fun without you guys," I say. "Every time we did something, I wished you two were there to share it with."

I pause before saying the most difficult sentence.

"I'm really sorry." I fiddle with my phone as I speak. "I know we planned to go to the fair together - I shouldn't have ditched you for Tiffany's party."

"Thanks to you, Kevin wouldn't stop following us around," Billy says. "Dot loved it."

Dot bats her eyes. "Turns out his friends ditched him to go camping."

"I guess it's going around," I add.

And just like that, my two best friends and I are back to our old selves.

"Let's go have some REAL fun." Billy hands me the huge stuffed pony. "Just the four of us."

"Annie! Dot! Billy!" Kevin holds a giant bag full of stuffed animals. "Can I hang with you guys?"

I look to Dot and Billy for a response. We all say yes.

"Race you to the Ferris wheel," SAM says.

We spend the next few hours riding the Ferris Wheel, Bumper Cars, and Tilt-a-Whirl, and play carnival games until SAM reaches the prize-winning limit. We eat cotton candy, corn on the cob, and deep fried candy bars. At the animal pavilion, we even get to milk cows.

Kevin is about to squirt us with milk from the cow's udder until we stare him down and he changes his mind.

I feel someone tap my shoulder as I milk.

"I'm so glad to see you guys," Tiffany says. "Sorry about my boring party - my mom planned it like I was turning two."

"You guys look like you're having WAY more fun." When Austin adjusts his giant cowboy hat, I think Dot might be in love again.

Billy tilts the cow's udder and squirts Kevin in the eye with milk.

"You are hilarious," Zoe tells him.

"So I've been told." Billy shoots milk at Austin, prompting Dot to push him off his stool.

"Mind if we hang out with you guys?" Tiffany points to her more than dozen friends.

All of us ride, eat, and play games until dusk. Tiffany even lets Billy try on her tiara, wiping it down with hand sanitizer after he gives it back.

Of course Kevin couldn't behave himself forever and ties Fran's and Fern's shoelaces together while they wait in line for candied apples.

Tiffany offers to take me home in the limo, but I choose to ride home with Dot and Billy instead. The three of us pass out in the back of Billy's mom car, too stuffed and tired to move.

#ANewStar

It's not like Dot, Billy, and I hang out with Tiffany and her friends all the time now, but we DID have a fun afternoon together. It's a little less awkward when we see Tiffany in the halls and when it's time for MY birthday party, I'll probably invite her, Zoe, and Austin too. The best part is that Dot, Billy, and I are back on solid ground.

At dinner, all Dad can talk about is the great deal he negotiated with several pillow companies to turn our emoji faces into decorative objects for people's beds. The big surprise is that the image the pillow companies want most of all this season isn't Kevin's devilish grin or my smiling face, but Billy's.

"Are you saying the biggest selling pillow is poop?" My mother scoops mystery meat onto her plate.

"They're selling like hotcakes," Dad says. "Your friend Billy is a star!"

For a moment I feel a twinge of envy - why do people want accessories of Billy and not me? Not to be mean, but let's face it - he's POOP. I pull out my phone to check the latest emoji meter readings; sure enough, Billy's smiling face now graces the first slot.

"That's how it should be," Mom says. "Everybody gets a chance to be on top. Very democratic."

A wave of relief washes over me and I finally understand what Dot and Billy have known all along - the freedom that comes from not caring about being popular is BETTER than being popular.

I help Mom clear the table but my phone dings on the counter with a dozen new texts. They're from Billy and Dot, laughing at how ridiculous the new rankings are. Almost as ridiculous as me thinking I could find a better pair of friends than Dot and Billy.

I put down the stack of plates and join in the group text. And for the rest of the night, the smile on my face couldn't be more real.

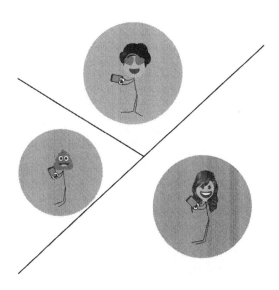

#IntroducingStinkySteve

Book 1: Minecraft Mishap
Book 2: Minecraft Superhero

#BooksInTheSeries

<u>Horse Party</u> * <u>Emoji Olympics</u>
<u>Call of Doodie</u> * <u>Reality TV</u>

#MakeaCameo

Want to be a Character in the next Emoji Adventures Book? Enter at:
www.EmojiAdventuresBook.com

#AlsobyPTEvans

App Mash-up Vol 1: Minecraft & Angry Birds
App Mash Vol. 2: Candy Crush & Fruit Ninja

#MorebyPTEvans

Minecat: A Feline Minecraft Adventure

Book One: A Whole Lot of Ocelots
Book Two: Sugar Cane Rush

Connect with PT Evans

Twitter: @PTEvansAuthor
Instagram: @PTEvansAuthor
Facebook: facebook.com/PTEvansAuthor

Twitter: @MontageBooks
Instagram: @MontagePublishing
Facebook:
facebook.com/montagepublishing
www.MontagePublishing.com

BONUS!

We have a FREE Book waiting for you...
www.montagepublishing.com/free-book-club

Made in the USA
Lexington, KY
08 February 2017